WHERE THE WILD THINGS ARE

HarperFestival is an imprint of HarperCollins Publishers.

Where the Wild Things Are: The Movie Storybook
© 2009 Warner Bros. Entertainment, Inc. All rights reserved.
Adapted by Barb Bersche and Michelle Quint
Printed in the United States of America.
www.harpercollinschildrens.com
Library of Congress Cataloging-in-Publication Data is available.
ISBN 978-0-06-165686-6
09 10 11 12 13 LP/WOR 10 9 8 7 6 5 4 3 2 1
First Edition

HINGS ARE

Based on the screenplay by
Spike Jonze and Dave Eggers

Based on the book by
Maurice Sendak

Snow had fallen overnight. The next day,
Max built the world's best igloo. Flushed with
pride, he wanted his sister, Claire, to see it.
He had made it, after all, and it was masterful.
But Claire was too busy to bother with her
little brother.

   Max felt safe in his igloo. He packed snowball
after snowball, shaping each one just right.
He'd be ready when Claire's friends arrived.

Finally, a car pulled into the driveway and Claire's friends spilled out.

Giddy with anticipation, Max hurled the first snowball, catching them off guard. But snowballs came back at him in a rapid flurry. He couldn't control the attack. Max bolted into his igloo for cover but Claire's friends didn't stop. An arm smashed through the side, searching for Max. They jumped onto the roof, crushing his amazing igloo and burying Max in the snow.

Max ran into the house, embarrassed and angry that Claire had done nothing to help him. He went to Claire's room and ripped up the valentine he made her last year. That'll show her! But when he was done, he felt worse instead of better.

When Max's mom came home, Max told her what happened with Claire and her friends. Then he showed her the mess he'd made in her room. Max's mom understood why he was upset. But he still saw her face crinkle with worry.

Later that night, Max tiptoed into
his mom's office, where she was working
on her computer. He wanted to see if she
was upset about Claire's room.

"I feel like a story," she said to Max.

This was a game they played together
sometimes—Max would think of a story
and she'd type along with him.

"There were some buildings . . . there
were these really tall buildings . . . and
they could walk. . . . Then there were
some vampires . . ." he began. When his
story was over, his mom smiled and Max
knew everything was okay.

Usually, Max daydreamed in school, but not today. "The solar system," his teacher said, "will go dark . . . permanently." This troubled Max.

When he got home, Max built a spectacular fort out of blankets. "Mom, Mom, come up here!" Max shouted excitedly.

"I'm busy," she shouted back.

First his sister ignored his
igloo, and now his mom was
ignoring his fort. Max looked
unhappily around his bedroom
for something fun to do.

Aha! His wolf suit! He
grabbed it from the back of the
door and put it on. Strutting
into the kitchen, Max felt strong
and sure.

ut Max's mom still wasn't paying attention to him. She was busy making dinner. Max became angry and frustrated. He couldn't stop himself from acting how he felt: like an animal.

"Max, get off the counter," his mom said sternly. Max growled back. His mom chased him into the front hall and grabbed him. Before he could stop himself, Max bit down on her arm. "Ouch!" his mom cried. Max had no idea what to do, so he turned and ran out of the house.

Max ran through the dark night, down
the road and into the forest. He felt wild.
He grabbed a stick and stomped around,
whacking a tree. He howled into the sky
and the wind howled back. He saw the stars
reflected in the water near his feet and heard
the sound of a boat knocking against the
shore. Without another thought, Max stepped
in and the boat slowly drifted away.

Max sailed for many days and nights
without seeing land. Finally, a curious orange
glow appeared in the distance—an island!
He saw the light was coming from a giant fire.
Though Max was exhausted, he managed to
drag his boat ashore. Seeking warmth
and food, he ventured toward the fire.

Crouching behind the trees, Max saw six enormous creatures by the fire. He was confused, but felt a strange excitement stirring inside him. One creature leaped about, destroying round, nestlike structures, while the rest grunted and squealed and argued.

Their bodies were gigantic. They had long
claws and fantastically sharp teeth. These were
wild things, full of mischief, and Max wanted badly
to join in their fun.

"Gaaaaaah yahhhhh!" Max burst through the forest and into the open. He began imitating the creature named Carol by bashing in the walls of one of the circular huts. Carol was happy but the others were less enthusiastic about a strange boy tearing into their buildings.

"Hey, what are you doing?" said the creature named Douglas.

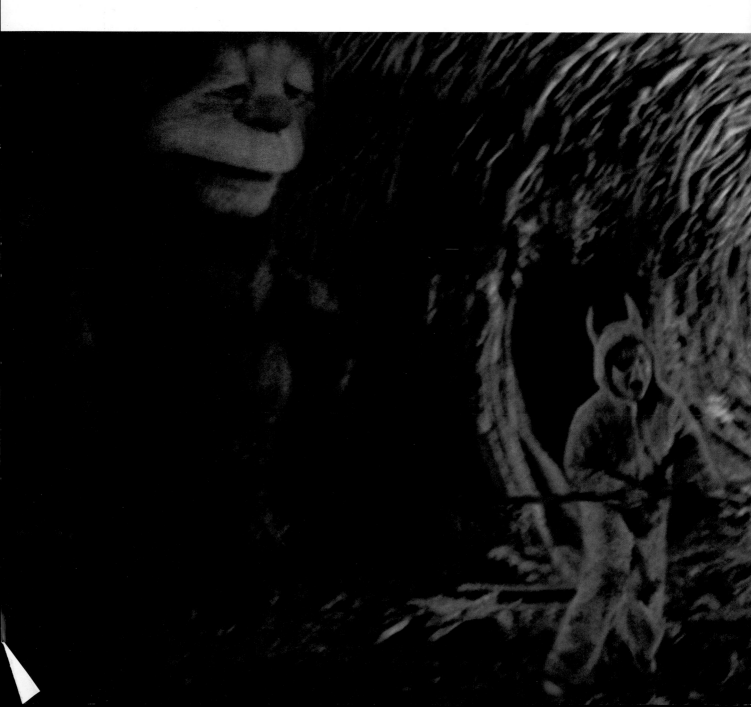

"I'm just helping," said Max.

"By smashing our houses?" Douglas answered.

Max grew nervous.

"You know what I say, if you've got a problem, eat it," said Judith, who had a sharp horn at the end of her nose.

The creatures encircled Max, gnashing their teeth, gleefully ready to devour him.

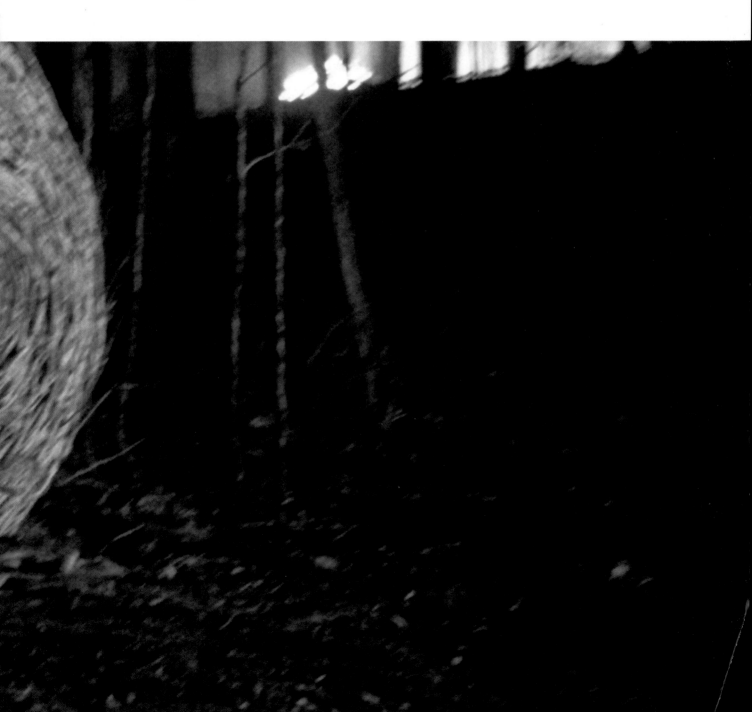

"Beeeeee stilllll!" Max yelled.

"Why?" asked the creatures.

Max threw his arms up and stared at the creatures like he was casting a spell. To his surprise, it worked.

"Because you can't eat me. You didn't know that, so I forgive you. But don't try it again," he said.

Max quickly invented a story about how he once defeated a band of Vikings who attacked him in his ice fortress.

"Are you a king?" asked Carol, the largest of the wild things.

"Yes, I am," declared Max.

"Sorry we were going to eat you," the creature named Ira said. "We didn't realize you were king."

Carol put a crown on Max's head.

"We got a king," Carol said. "Everything's going to be different."

They lifted Max up and shouted, "King! King! King!"

Carol said, "Hey, King! What's your first order of business?"

Max answered immediately. "Let the wild rumpus start!"

Running through the forest, the wild things competed for
Max's attention, performing any task that he commanded.
They shrieked, they jumped, they danced, and they howled.
Max loved every minute. He could never do this at home!

Finally, exhausted and happy from the rumpus,
they all fell asleep in one big pile.

When Max awoke, he realized
he was being carried in Carol's arms.
He climbed atop Carol's head to
get a better view. They walked through
the dense forest and across the
sand dunes.

"Everything you see is yours,"
Carol announced. "I want you to be
king forever."

At first, Max agreed. But a few
minutes later, he thought about what
forever meant.

"Did you know the sun is going
to die?" he asked Carol.

"Oh, come on. That can't happen.
You're the king! And look at me.
I'm big. How can guys like us worry
about a little thing like the sun?"
Carol assured him.

hey arrived at Carol's secret workshop.
Inside, Max discovered a miniature city with a
river flowing through it. It was a perfect model
world that Carol had constructed.

wish I could live in there," said Max longingly.
    "Yeah, it was gonna be a place where only
things you wanted to have happen would
happen," Carol agreed. He looked down sadly at
his beautiful creation.
    Max thought for a minute. "Carol, we can
build a real place like that!" Max said.

Carol and Max walked back to tell the rest of the wild things about the amazing fort they would build. "It's going to be as tall as twelve of you and six of me," cried Max.

"And only we can get in. We can have an ice cream parlor. A swimming pool with a bottom that is a trampoline," Max said.

Even Judith, usually the most grumpy creature, was excited about the project.

The fort was taking shape and all the wild things were cheerfully working together. Carol carved a heart shape into a beam, with an "M" in the center, for Max.

The creatures and Max worked day and night on the fort. Things were going great! Rocks got piled up high to make the walls. Sticks were woven together. The fort was perfect.

The wild things played well together, but still, there were occasional problems. Judith told Max that she thought he was playing favorites. This really bothered Max. He was trying so hard to be a good king.

After the creature called K.W. saw that Judith upset Max, she took him for a walk to find some sticks in the desert. K.W. always knew how to make Max feel better. She suggested that he talk to two of her good friends, a pair of owls named Bob and Terry. "Seriously," she told him, "they're really smart. They have the answers to everything."

Max agreed to let K.W. bring the owls back
to the fort, but when they arrived, Max immediately
knew it was a mistake.

Carol didn't like the owls. He turned to Max
and said, "I thought you said if anybody got in
here we didn't want, the fort would automatically
cut their brains out."

Max began to worry. As king, it was his job to keep the peace. All he wanted was for K.W. and Carol to be friends. Why was it so hard? He had to think of something else to do to distract them, and fast.

"We're going to have a war!" Max declared.

"Hmmm," Judith said.

"It's the best way to have fun together," Max insisted. He chose teams of good guys and bad guys. But before Max could explain the rules, he was hit by a giant ball of dirt.

"Look out for the bad guys!" squealed Ira. The war
had begun. Dirt clods were exploding from all sides.
    But soon the fun turned into something else.
Douglas hit Alexander too hard, Carol threw a raccoon
at Ira's nose, and K.W. stepped on Carol's head.
Suddenly, everyone was angry and upset.

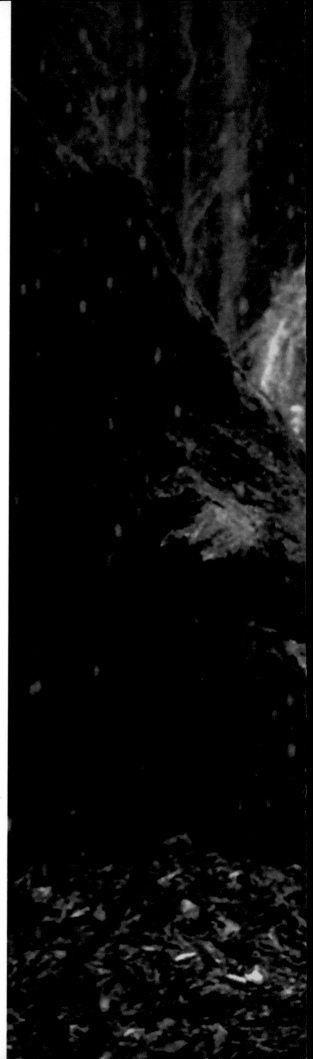

"So, King. What's going on? This is how you rule a kingdom? Everyone fighting? The bad guys feel bad. Everyone feels bad!" exclaimed Judith.

The wild things sat around the fire, taking turns grumbling at Max. Finally Carol said, "He'll keep us together. He has powers. Right? Show us."

Max stood up, as the group stared and waited for him to do something. He did the only thing he could think of: his robot dance.

The wild things, dumbfounded and disappointed, walked off. Max was all alone. He stared into the darkness, unsure of what to do next.

That night, Carol couldn't sleep. Nothing in his world was as it seemed—Max wasn't acting like a king, not at all, not even a little. Everything was wrong! He began to panic.

Carol couldn't keep his bad feelings inside.
He woke everyone up, announcing that they had to
destroy the fort. "It's all wrong!" he cried.

He was convinced that the sun was dead, and
that the fort was a failure.

"You're a terrible king," Carol told Max.

"He's not a king," Douglas said.

Carol was stunned. Max wasn't even a king?

"I'll eat you up!" roared Carol, chasing Max
into the woods.

Max raced through the forest as fast as possible, but Carol was close behind, growling ferociously.

Desperate to save him, K.W. snatched Max from his path and swallowed him whole, hiding him deep inside her belly before Carol would notice.

"I just wanted us all to be together," Carol sadly told K.W., not realizing Max could hear him. Even though Max was scared of Carol, he felt bad for him, too.

"Do you believe him?" K.W. asked Max
when Carol walked away.

Max did. "He loves you," he told her.
"You're his family."

K.W. thought for moment. "Yeah," she
said. "It's hard being a family."

And as K.W. pulled Max out of her throat
and he again saw the sky and the ground,
he knew it was time to leave the island. He
needed to go home. He needed to figure out
how to be a better part of his own family.

Max returned to his boat on the beach. The other wild things joined him there, with long, sad faces, unsure of what to say.

"You're the first king we haven't eaten," said Judith.

"It's true," added Alexander.

"Don't go, Max," K.W. begged. "I'll eat you up, I love you so."

Max gave them each a hug good-bye and then climbed
into his boat. As he drifted off, Carol appeared on the
beach, looking very sorry. He waded out into the ocean.

"Arrrooo!" Max howled gently to his friend Carol.

"Arrrooo!" Carol howled back to Max.

"Arrrooo!" the other wild things joined in, as Max
floated away and disappeared into the night.

Max sailed, determined to find his way home. After a long while, he saw a forest and the twinkling city lights. He was so close!

He docked his boat and ran as fast as he could, back through the forest and his streets. Neighborhood dogs barked at him, and he barked back.

He knew there was a part of him that loved being wild, but he knew he had to be a boy, too—a boy who desperately missed his mom and sister.

When Max reached his house, he hesitated. What if his mom was still mad at him? But when Max's mom saw him, she grabbed him and hugged him tight. Max sat down at the table, where his dinner was waiting for him.

He was finally home.